nine witch tales

Edited by Abby Kedabra

Illustrated by John Fernie

SCHOLASTIC BOOK SERVICES

NEW YORK • TORONTO • LONDON • AUCKLAND • SYDNEY

For reprint permission grateful acknowledgment is made to:

Mrs. Robert A. Leflar for "The Hungry Old Witch" from TALES FROM SILVER LANDS by Charles J. Finger, copyright 1924 by Charles J. Finger.

Thomas Nelson & Sons for "Baba Yaga" from OLD PETER'S RUSSIAN TALES by Arthur Ransome, copyright 1917 by Arthur Ransome.

Roy Publishers, Inc., for "The Bewitching Ointment" from a BREW OF WITCH-CRAFT by Geoffrey Palmer and Noel Lloyd, © 1966 by Geoffrey Palmer and Noel Lloyd; "The Horned Witches" and "The Witch of Wandaland" from JOURNEY BY BROOMSTICK by Geoffrey Palmer and Noel Lloyd, © 1966 by Geoffrey Palmer and Noel Lloyd.

Vanguard Press, Inc., for "The Young Witch-Horse" and "The Hex and the Oxen" from UPSTATE, DOWNSTATE: FOLK TALES OF THE MIDDLE AT-LANTIC STATES by M. Jagendorf, copyright 1949 by M. Jagendorf.

World Publishing Company for "The Cat Witch" from THE THING AT THE FOOT OF THE BED AND OTHER SCARY TALES by Maria Leach, © 1959 by Maria Leach.

1st printing . . . . September 1968

Printed in the U.S.A.

CONTENTS

Witch's Chant

Double, double, toil and trouble,
Fire burn and cauldron bubble.
Round about the cauldron go!
In the poisoned entrails throw:
Fillet of a fenny snake,
In the cauldron boil and bake;
Eye of newt and toe of frog,
Wool of bat and tongue of dog,
Adder's fork and blindworm's sting,
Lizard's leg and owlet's wing;
Thrice to thine, and thrice to mine,
And thrice again to make up nine!

— from *Macbeth* by William Shakespeare

The
Horned
Witches

THERE WAS ONCE AN OLD WOMAN who lived with her only daughter in a cottage at the foot of a mountain in County Tipperary.

Pegeen, the daughter, was soon to be married to Patrick Ennis from the other side of the mountain. He was a well-to-do farmer, so the old woman wanted Pegeen to have a trousseau that would be the envy of all the neighbors, and would show that the folk on their side of the mountain were as good as those on the other.

Night after night, after Pegeen had gone to bed, she sat by the dying fire, stitching away at bridal gown, veil, tablecloths, towels, sheets, and napkins, until her head ached and her eyes were sore.

When the wedding was only a week away and there was still much to be done, the old woman grew anxious for fear things would not be ready on the day. She stayed up later than ever, hardly able to see her needle and thread, so faint was the glimmer from the last few embers on the hearth. "I wish there was somebody to help me," she thought. "I could not bear the disgrace if everything is not ready."

Suddenly there was a knock at the cottage door, and a voice called, "Open, open!"

"Who can that be at this early hour?" the old woman asked herself, and felt nervous as she called in a quavering voice, "Who is there?"

"I am the Witch of the One Horn," was the answer.

Thinking she had not heard aright and that one of the neighbors needed help, the old woman hobbled to the door and opened it. Standing on the threshold, tall and lean in the moonlight, and wrapped in a long black cloak, was a woman she had never seen before.

"What do you want of me?" Pegeen's mother began, but the stranger pushed past her and strode into the room. She went straight to a chair by the fire, took up a needle and thread, and began to hem a tablecloth with hasty, jerky movements. Not a word did she speak, and it was not until the old woman had returned to her own seat and taken up her needle that she noticed, growing out of the stranger's forehead, a short, curved horn.

"The Witch of the One Horn," she thought, and a stab of fear went through her. "Has she come to help me, or has she another purpose?" And her fingers shook.

The witch finished the tablecloth in a miraculously short time and took up another piece of material. She spoke for the first time, as if to herself. "Where are the women? They are very late."

Immediately there was another knock at the door, and a voice called, "Open, open!"

The old woman glanced timidly at her companion, wondering whether or not to answer the call, but the witch was bent over her work, so she opened the door.

Standing on the threshold was another woman, even taller and leaner than the first, and covered from head to foot in black. She took no notice of the old woman, but went straight into the room and took a seat next to her sister witch. She picked up a needle and thread and began to hem a sheet. She did not speak, and when the old woman had reached her own seat she noticed that the newcomer had two horns growing out of her forehead.

In the silence that followed, the old woman thought the beating of her heart must be as loud as the ticking of a grandfather clock, but the Witch of the One Horn and the Witch of the Two Horns continued to stitch away, their needles stabbing like lightning at the fine linen.

Suddenly the second witch said, "Where are the other women? There is still much work to do." She was answered by a knock on the door and the same peremptory call.

And so the knocks went on, and each time Pegeen's mother, not daring to ignore the knocks, answered the door, another witch strode in and took a seat. Each witch had one more horn than the one before, and when the last one had entered and taken up her sewing the old woman counted twelve short, curved horns growing from her forehead.

The old woman did not know what to do. She saw the pile of tablecloths, sheets, and towels grow, but even the knowledge that everything would be ready for the wedding did not comfort her. The flickering light played on the ugly faces and spare forms of her twelve visitors, and the horns on their foreheads glowed with a strange, luminous light. "Will they go when they have finished their tasks?" she wondered. "Should I offer them some refreshment? Surely they will go away when morning comes. . . ."

Her own sewing grew slower, the stitches longer and more uneven. She saw to her dismay that she had made a crooked hem on Pegeen's new petticoat. It would all have to be ripped out and done again. She sighed and reached for her scissors.

At that moment the twelve witches began to sing a wordless tune that was full of an eerie, haunting horror, making the old woman's skin to prickle and her hair to rise. "What next?" she thought. "What evil thing is about to happen?"

She tried to get up, to call out, but found she could do neither. She was bound to her chair, enclosed in a spell that the song had woven. A thin, swirling mist crept into the room and made everything hazy. Through the mist the witches seemed to dissolve, then become solid again, fading and growing until the old woman's head swam.

The Witch of the One Horn swayed toward her in the strange gloom. Her eyes, glowing like rubies, glared into the old woman's. "Old woman," she crooned, "rise and make us a cake. We have worked hard and long, and we are hungry."

"Make us a cake. We are hungry," came a whisper from the others.

As if in a dream, the old woman got up. She

groped her way to the shelf where she kept her pots and pans, and tried to lift down a mixing bowl. But it seemed to be stuck to the shelf and she could not move it. She tried to get another, then another, but none of them would come away. She let her hands fall helplessly to her sides and turned to the witches. "Will they kill me for disobeying?" she thought dully.

The Witch of the Twelve Horns got up and advanced toward her. From her eyes flashed a fire as green as emeralds. "Old woman," she hissed, "take a sieve to the well and bring water in it to mix with the flour to make the cake."

"Take a sieve to the well," the others sighed.

There was a sieve hanging from a nail near the door. Blindly the old woman reached out for it, took it down, and somehow found herself outside the cottage and dragging herself to the well at the bottom of the garden.

There the nightmare continued. Every time she drew water into the sieve, it poured through the holes and splashed on the ground. "I will never do it," the old woman panted. "I will never get the cake made, and they will kill me." She threw down the sieve, sat by the well, and wept bitterly.

A low, clear voice pierced her misery. It floated up from the depths of the well and fell on her ears like a cool balm. "Take some yellow clay and some moss," it said, "and bind them together. Then put it round the sieve and the sieve will hold water."

Still in a trance, the old woman stumbled to her feet and saw that on one side of the well was a patch of wet clay and on the other side a bed of soft moss. She gathered a handful of each, mixed them together, and plastered the sieve with the sticky mixture. Then she drew some water and was overjoyed to find that this time it did not dribble away. "Thank you," she whispered to the well.

Then the voice came again, bubbling up as sweet and cool as a mountain spring. "Do what I say and all will be well. When you get to the door, stand on the threshold and cry out in a loud voice, 'The mountain is on fire and the sky is blood-red!' Do this three times, then stand to one side."

Carefully holding the sieve so that the water did not spill, the old woman returned to her cottage. She put the sieve on the ground, opened the door, and, her voice cracking with anxious hope, called out, "The mountain is on fire and the sky is blood-red!"

She waited. Nothing happened, but the silence in the room quivered into life. She called again, and waited. The silence stirred as though a multitude of little things were on the move. When she had called out the words for the third time, she moved away from the open door.

From inside the cottage came a terrible cry, as if beasts had been made angry by desperate wounds. Out rushed the twelve witches, and the air shivered and splintered with their wild lamentations and piercing shrieks. They rose from the ground like giant bats, their black cloaks flapping, and they soared up into the night sky, twisting and turning in their frantic desire to get back to their home on the mountain before it was devoured by fire.

The old woman watched them getting smaller and smaller, until they became black dots and finally disappeared. As soon as they had gone, the dawn broke and birds began to sing.

The old woman's heart was full of thankfulness. Before going inside, she turned back to the well. "Thank you, oh thank you, spirit of the well," she murmured. "You have saved me from the terrible horned women."

The spirit of the well spoke again, warningly. "The witches will come back when they find that the mountain is not on fire. If they enter your house a second time, you and your daughter will never be seen alive again. You must prepare your home against their enchantment. Listen, this is what you must do. . . ."

The old woman nodded as she listened to the soft, bubbling words. Then she went back to the cottage, her eyes bright with resolve, her step firm with courage.

She took water from the sieve and sprinkled it over the doorstep. When she got inside she saw a cake, dark reddish-brown and unappetizing to look at, on the table. "They didn't even wait for me to come back with the water," she said to herself. "They were greedy as well as wicked. But thanks to the spirit of the well I know what is in that cake."

She broke it into pieces, kept one in her hand and threw the others into the hearth, where they sizzled for a moment, then shriveled up into hard black lumps. She went up the twisting stairs to the tiny room where her daughter slept, and bent over the still form in the narrow bed.

Pegeen's hair spread over the pillow like a fan of black lace. Her face was as white as the pillow she lay on; her lips were bloodless. One blue-veined hand rested on the counterpane. The old woman smoothed the girl's brow. "I would have thought you dead," she whispered, "if the spirit had not told me how the witches took your blood to mix with flour for their cake. Here is your life back again, dear daughter." And she touched the girl's lips with the piece of cake.

Pegeen stirred and sighed. The color flowed back into her cheeks, the red into her lips. When the old woman saw that she was sleeping normally, she gave a sigh of happiness and tiptoed out of the room.

Downstairs, she closed the door and made it secure with a great crossbeam fastened between the jambs. Then, sitting by the hearth, she took up her sewing and waited.

A sound like a hurricane battering against the stout walls of the cottage told her that the twelve witches had returned. There was such a banging and a shouting, such a bawling and a screaming, that she thought the walls would cave in. The door shuddered under the onslaught, the windows rattled, the very foundations trembled.

"Open, open!" the witches screeched. "Vengeance, vengeance!" they howled.

The old woman waited behind the barred door, her hands clasped, her breathing tremulous, her body shrinking into the shadows.

Then a single voice rose above the hubbub. "Open, open, well water!"

The water that had been sprinkled on the doorstep made a murmuring answer. "I cannot open — I am scattered on the step and on the ground, and I cannot open for you."

A second voice jarred the air. "Open, open, wood and beam!"

The door, straining against the crossbeam, grunted, "I cannot open — a beam is fixed between my jambs, and I cannot open for you."

Then all twelve voices rose in a menacing roar. "Open, open, cake that we have made and mingled with blood!"

From the hearth came a sighing reply. "I cannot open — I am broken and burned, and my blood is back in the sleeping girl. I cannot open for you."

The noise dissolved into a long drawn-out moan, and the witches started to wring their hands and curse the spirit of the well that had wrecked their plans and saved the lives of the old woman and her daughter. But when they realized that nothing they could do would have any effect on the magic stronger than theirs, they flew away in rage.

So the valley was left in peace, and the wedding preparations were able to go forward without fear of interruption. Pegeen married her Patrick, and all the guests were amazed at the great quantity of exquisitely sewn dresses and linen on display. "How did you manage to do so much in such a short time?" they asked.

But the old woman only smiled and said, "Oh, I had a little help toward the end. . . ."

The
Huntsman
and the
Witch

ONE FINE DAY, many years ago, a brave young man went into the forest to hunt. He was gay and light-hearted, and he whistled a tune as he went along.

Suddenly an ugly old crone spoke to him and said, "Good morning, dear huntsman. You are merry and happy enough, while I am hungry and thirsty. Pray give me a coin."

The huntsman pitied the poor woman. He put his hand in his pocket and made her a present of a silver coin.

Then he wanted to go on, but the old woman held him back and said, "Hark ye, dear huntsman,

I will now give *you* a present, because of your good heart. Go on your way and you will come to a tree on which nine birds are sitting. They will have a cloak in their claws, over which they are fighting. Take aim with your gun and shoot into the middle of them. They will drop the cloak, and one of the birds will fall down dead. Take the cloak with you. It is a wishing cloak. When you throw it round your shoulders you have only to wish yourself at a place to be there at once. Take the heart out of the dead bird and swallow it whole. Then you will find a gold coin under your pillow every single morning when you wake."

The huntsman thanked the wise woman and thought, "She promises fine things. If only they turn out as well!"

When he had gone about a hundred paces he heard above him, in the branches of a tree, such a chattering and screaming that he looked up. There he saw a flock of birds pulling at a garment with their beaks and claws. They were snatching and tearing at it as if each one wanted to have it for himself.

"Well," said the huntsman, "this is extraordinary. It is exactly as the old woman said."

He put his gun to his shoulder, took aim, and

fired right into the middle of them, making the feathers fly about. The birds took flight with a great noise, all except one, which fell dead, and the cloak dropped at his feet.

He did as the old woman had told him: he cut the heart out of the bird and swallowed it whole. Then he took the cloak home with him. When he woke in the morning he remembered the old woman's promise, and looked under his pillow to see if all was true. There, sure enough, lay a golden coin. The next morning he found another, and then another, each morning, until he had collected quite a pile of gold. At last he thought, "What is the good of all my gold if I stay at home here? I will go out into the world and look about." So he shouldered his gun and started off.

One day he came to a thick forest, and when he had gone through it he saw a fine castle. An old woman was standing in one of the windows looking out, and a beautiful golden-haired maiden stood beside her.

But the old woman was a witch, and she said to the maiden, "Here comes someone out of the forest. He has a wonderful treasure inside him. We must try to get it from him, my darling. It will suit us better than him. He has a bird's heart about him, and therefore he finds a gold coin every morning under his pillow when he wakes."

She told the girl how he had got it and at last said, "If you don't get it from him it will be the worse for you."

When the huntsman drew nearer, he saw the maiden and thought, "I have been wandering about a long time. I will go into this castle and rest."

He went in, and he was kindly received and hospitably treated. Before long he fell so in love with the maiden that he thought of nothing else and cared for nothing but pleasing her.

Then the witch said to the maiden, "Now we must get the bird's heart. He will never miss it."

She concocted a potion, and when it was ready she put it into a goblet. The maiden took it to him and said, "Now, my beloved, you must drink to me."

He took the cup and drank the potion, and when he was overpowered by it, the bird's heart came out of his mouth. The maiden took it away secretly and swallowed it herself, as the old witch had bid her.

From this time on the huntsman found no more gold under his pillow. The coin was always under the maiden's instead, and the old woman used to fetch it away every morning. But the huntsman was so much in love that he thought only of enjoying himself in the maiden's company.

Then the old witch said, "We have the bird's heart, but we must have his wishing cloak too."

The maiden said, "Let us leave him that. We have taken away his wealth."

But the old woman was very angry and said, "A cloak like that is a very wonderful thing. Have it I must and will." So the maiden obeyed the witch's orders. She sat herself at the window, and looked sadly out at the distant range of hills.

The huntsman asked, "Why are you so sad?"

"Alas, my love," was her answer, "over there are the garnet mountains, where precious stones are found. I long for them so much that I grow sad whenever I think of them. But who could ever get them? The birds that fly, perhaps. No mortal could ever reach them."

"If that is all your trouble," said the huntsman, "I can soon lift that load from your heart."

Then he drew her under his cloak and in a moment they were both sitting on the mountain. The precious stones were glittering around them. Their hearts rejoiced at the sight of them and they soon gathered together some of the finest and largest.

Now the witch had worked a spell that made the

huntsman feel very drowsy. So he said to the maiden, "Let us sit down to rest awhile, for I am so tired I can stand no longer."

They sat down, and the huntsman laid his head on her lap and slept. As soon as he was asleep, the maiden slipped the cloak from his shoulders and put it on. Then she loaded herself with precious garnets, and wished herself back at the castle.

The huntsman slept a long time. When he woke up, he saw that his beloved had betrayed him and left him alone on the wild mountain.

"Oh, what treachery is in the world!" he exclaimed, as he sat down in grief. He did not know what to do.

Now the mountain belonged to some wild and savage giants who lived on it, and before long the huntsman saw three of them striding along. He quickly lay down again and pretended to be fast asleep.

The first one, as he came along, stumbled against him and said, "What kind of earthworm is this?"

The second said, "Tread on him and kill him."

But the third said, "It isn't worth the trouble. Let him alone. He can't live here, and when he climbs higher up the mountain the clouds will roll down and carry him off."

The huntsman heard all that they said, and as soon as they were gone he got up and climbed to the top of the mountain. After he had sat there for a time, a cloud floated over him and carried him away. At first he was swept through the air, but then he was gently lowered and deposited within a large walled garden, upon a soft bed of lettuce and other herbs.

He looked around him and said, "If only I had something to eat. I am so hungry! But I see neither apples nor pears nor any other fruit — nothing but salad and herbs."

At last, however, he thought, "At least, I can eat some of this salad. Even if it does not taste good it will be refreshing."

He picked out a fine head of lettuce and began eating it. But he had hardly swallowed a little piece when he began to feel very odd and quite changed. He felt four legs growing, a big head, and two long ears, and he saw to his horror that he was changed into an ass.

He still felt as hungry as ever and the juicy salad was now very much to his taste, so he went on eating. At last he reached another kind of salad, which he had hardly tasted when he felt a new change taking place, and found himself back in his human shape. After this he lay down and slept off his fatigue.

When he woke next morning he broke off a head of the bad salad and a head of the good. He put the salad into his wallet, climbed over the wall, and went off to find the witch's castle.

After wandering about for a few days, he was fortunate enough to find it. Then he stained his face and disguised himself so that his own mother would not have known him, and went to the castle to ask for shelter.

"I am so tired," he said. "I cannot go any farther."

The witch said, "Who are you, countryman, and what do you want?"

He answered, "I am a messenger from the King. He sent me to find the rarest salad that grows under the sun. I have been lucky enough to find it, and I carry it with me. But the sun is so burning hot that I am afraid the tender plant will be withered, and I don't know if I shall be able to take it any farther."

When the old witch heard about the rare salad, she felt a great desire to have some and said, "Good countryman, let me try the wonderful salad."

"By all means," he answered. "I have two heads

with me and you shall have one." So saying, he opened his sack and handed her the bad one.

The witch had no suspicions, and her mouth so watered for the new dish that she went to the kitchen herself to prepare it. When it was ready, she could not wait till it was put on the table, but put a few leaves into her mouth at once. Hardly had she swallowed them when she lost her human shape, and she ran out into the courtyard as an old she-ass.

Then the kitchen maid came in and saw the salad standing ready, and was about to put it on the table. But on the way, she decided to taste it, and ate a few leaves. Immediately she too turned into an ass, and ran out into the yard to join the old witch. The dish of salad fell to the ground.

"This is all right," said the huntsman. "Two of them are done for." Then he picked up the leaves, put them on a dish, and took them to the maiden.

"I am bringing the precious food to you myself," said he, "so that you will not have to wait any longer."

She ate some, and like the others was immediately changed into an ass, and ran out to them in the yard.

When the huntsman had washed his face so that

the creatures might know him, he went into the courtyard and said, "Now you shall be paid for your treachery."

He tied all three asses together with a rope and drove them along to the mill. He tapped at the window, and the miller put his head out and asked what he wanted.

"I have three bad animals here," said the huntsman. "I want to get rid of them. If you will take them and treat them as I wish, I will pay whatever you ask."

"How do you want them treated?" said the miller.

The huntsman said he wanted the old she-ass (the witch) to be well beaten three times a day and fed once, and the younger one (the maid) to be beaten once and fed three times. The youngest of all, who was the beautiful maiden, was to be fed three times and not beaten at all. He could not find it in his heart to have her beaten. Then he went back to the castle.

A few days later the miller came and told him that the old ass which was to be beaten three times and fed once was dead. "The other two," he said, "which were to be fed three times, are not dead, but they are pining away and won't last long."

The huntsman's heart was stirred with pity and he told the miller to bring them back to him. When they came he gave them some of the other salad to eat, so that they took their human shapes again. The beautiful maiden fell on her knees before him, and said, "Oh, my beloved, forgive me all the wrong I have done you. My stepmother, who was a witch, forced me to do it. It was against my own will, for I love you dearly. Your wishing cloak is hanging in the cupboard, and you shall have the bird's heart back too."

But he said, "Keep it. It will be all the same, as I will take you to be my own true wife."

Their marriage was soon after celebrated, and they lived long and happily together.

The
Cat
Witch

ONCE THERE WAS A YOUNG MAN named Kowashi, who lived with his old mother in a small Japanese village at the foot of the mountain. They were happy, respectable people and lived their lives in the simple, good way.

There was just one thing the young man used to wonder about. His mother used to be a gentle, sweet little woman. But when she got to be about eighty years old, he began to notice that she had long, sharp, pointed teeth. She used to eat her fish, tail, eyes, and all; she even seemed to enjoy crunching up the raw bones.

One night a fish peddler of Kowashi's village was walking home through the mountain pass after a day's work at the market. He had not sold all his fish that day. And those left over were in the fish basket which he carried on a pole over his shoulder.

He was not afraid of night robbers, because it was a bright moonlit night and he could see every stick and stone in the path.

Suddenly he was set upon by a whole horde of cats. They smelled the fish in his basket and were determined to get it.

He fought them off with the long pole. And he fought so smartly that finally the cats gave up the fight. Then one of them said, "Go call Old Woman Kowashi."

"That's funny," the peddler said to himself, for young Kowashi and his mother were his neighbors in the village.

So the man quickly climbed into a pine tree, wondering what would happen next.

In the moonlight the man could see the path and all the cats and their shadows as plain as day.

Soon one of the cats said, "Here she comes."

Another said, "Here comes Old Woman Kowashi."

The man looked. And what he saw was a big tough old gray cat coming through the pass.

"He won't give us the fish!" all the cats said together.

So the big gray cat climbed up into the fish peddler's tree. The peddler was lying stretched out along a branch. The cat crawled out along the same branch until she came close to him — eye to eye!

Inch by inch she came nearer. Each of her sharp claws looked six inches long.

What could he do?

Suddenly he remembered that he had his fish gaff with him. (A fish gaff is a heavy barbed hook with a wooden handle, used for hauling heavy fish into a boat.)

Quickly he grabbed the fish gaff and gave the big gray cat a whack on the head.

Just about then the sun peeked over the horizon. It was morning, and all the cats vanished instantly. One minute they were there, and the next minute they were gone — just like that.

The fish peddler climbed down from the tree and hurried home. And that morning he went and told young Kowashi the whole story.

The young man listened and nodded his head. He was thinking about how his mother had

changed, and how her teeth had gotten so pointed.
And just this morning he had noticed a deep gash
on her head.

Now he asked her how she had cut herself, and
she glared at him with baleful eyes and snarled,
baring her long pointed teeth.

So young Kowashi suddenly understood: a cat
witch had taken his mother's place! Quickly he
seized the witch, drew his long sword, and cut off
her head at one stroke.

Then he looked down, and what lay at his feet
was a bloody old gray cat!

Not long after this, Kowashi discovered that the
wicked cat witch had killed his real mother and
buried her in the garden.

Baba Yaga, the Forest Witch

ONCE UPON A TIME there was a widowed old man who lived alone in a hut with his little daughter. Very merry they were together, and they used to smile at each other over a table just piled with bread and jam. Everything went well until the old man took it into his head to marry again.

Yes, the old man became foolish in the years of his old age, and he took another wife. And so the poor little girl had a stepmother. And after that everything changed. There was no more bread and jam on the table, and no more playing peek-a-boo, first this side of the samovar and then that, as she sat with her father at tea. It was worse than that, for she never did sit at tea. The stepmother said that everything that went wrong was the little girl's fault. And the old man believed his new wife, and so there were no more kind words for his little daughter. Day after day the stepmother used to say that the little girl was too naughty to sit at table. And then she would throw her a crust and tell her to get out of the hut and go and eat it somewhere else.

And the poor little girl used to go away by herself into the shed in the yard, and wet the dry crust with her tears, and eat it all alone. Ah me! she often wept for the old days, and she often wept at the thought of the days that were to come.

Mostly she wept because she was all alone, until one day she found a little friend in the shed. She was hunched up in a corner of the shed, eating her crust and crying bitterly, when she heard a little noise. It was like this: scratch — scratch. It was a little gray mouse who lived in a hole.

Out he came, with his little pointed nose and his long whiskers, his little round ears and his bright eyes. Out came his little humpy body and his long tail. And then he sat up on his hind legs and curled his tail twice around himself and looked at the little girl.

The little girl, who had a kind heart, forgot all her sorrows and took a scrap of her crust and threw it to the little mouse. The mouseykin nibbled and nibbled, and there, it was gone, and he was looking for another. She gave him another bit, and presently that was gone, and another and another, until there was no crust left for the little girl. Well, she didn't mind that. You see, she was so happy seeing the little mouse nibbling and nibbling.

When the crust was gone, the mouseykin looks up at her with his little bright eyes, and "Thank you," he says in a little squeaky voice. "Thank you," he says. "You are a kind little girl, and I am only a mouse, and I've eaten all your crust. But there is one thing I can do for you, and that is to tell you to take care. The old woman in the hut [and that was the cruel stepmother] is the sister of Baba Yaga, the bony-legged, the witch. So if ever she sends you on an errand to your aunt, you come and tell me. For Baba Yaga would eat you soon enough with her iron teeth if you did not know what to do."

"Oh, thank you," said the little girl; and just then she heard the stepmother calling to her to come in and clean up the tea things, and tidy the house, and sweep the floor, and clean everybody's boots.

So off she had to go.

When she went in she had a good look at her stepmother. Sure enough she had a long nose, and she was as bony as a fish with all the flesh picked off, and the little girl thought of Baba Yaga and shivered, though she did not feel so bad when she remembered the mouseykin out there in the shed in the yard.

The very next morning it happened. The old man went off to pay a visit to some friends of his in the next village. And as soon as the old man was out of sight, the wicked stepmother called the little girl.

"You are to go today to your dear little aunt in the forest," says she, "and ask her for a needle and thread to mend a shirt."

"But here is a needle and thread," says the little girl.

"Hold your tongue," says the stepmother, and she gnashes her teeth, and they make a noise like clattering tongs. "Hold your tongue," she says. "Didn't I tell you you are to go today to your dear little aunt to ask for a needle and thread to mend a shirt?"

"How shall I find her?" says the little girl, nearly ready to cry, for she knew that her aunt was Baba Yaga, the bony-legged, the witch.

The stepmother took hold of the little girl's nose and pinched it.

"That is your nose," she says. "Can you feel it?"

"Yes," says the poor little girl.

"You must go along the road into the forest till you come to a fallen tree; then you must turn to your left and follow your nose, and you will find her," says the stepmother. "Now, be off with you, lazy one. Here is some food for you to eat by the way."

She gave the little girl a bundle wrapped up in a towel.

The little girl wanted to go into the shed to tell the mouseykin she was going to Baba Yaga, and to ask what she should do. But she looked back, and there was the stepmother at the door, watching her. So she had to go straight on.

She walked along the road through the forest till she came to the fallen tree. Then she turned to the left. Her nose was still hurting where the stepmother had pinched it, so she knew she had to go straight ahead. She was just setting out when she heard a little noise under the fallen tree.

"Scratch — scratch."

And out jumped the little mouse, and sat up in the road in front of her.

"O mouseykin, mouseykin," says the little girl,

"my stepmother has sent me to her sister. And that is Baba Yaga, the bony-legged, the witch, and I do not know what to do."

"It will not be difficult," says the little mouse, "because of your kind heart. Take all the things you find in the road and do with them what you like. Then you will escape from Baba Yaga and everything will be well."

"Are you hungry, mouseykin?" said the little girl.

"I could nibble, I think," says the little mouse.

The little girl unfastened the towel, and there was nothing in it but stones. That was what the stepmother had given the little girl to eat by the way.

"Oh, I'm so sorry," says the little girl. "There's nothing for you to eat."

"Isn't there?" said mouseykin, and as she looked at them, the little girl saw the stones turn to bread and jam. She sat down on the fallen tree, and the little mouse sat beside her, and they ate bread and jam until they were not hungry any more.

"Keep the towel," says the little mouse. "I think it will be useful. And remember what I said about the things you find on the way. And now good-bye," says he.

"Good-bye," says the little girl, and runs along.

As she was running along she found a nice new handkerchief lying in the road. She picked it up and took it with her. Then she found a little bottle of oil. She picked it up and took it with her. Then she found some scraps of meat.

"Perhaps I'd better take them too," she said, and she took them.

Then she found a gay blue ribbon, and she took that. Then she found a little loaf of good bread, and she took that too.

"I daresay somebody will like it," she said.

And then she came to the hut of Baba Yaga, the bony-legged, the witch. There was a high fence around it, with big gates. When she pushed them open, they squeaked miserably, as if it hurt them to move. The little girl was sorry for them.

"How lucky," she says, "that I picked up the bottle of oil!" and she poured the oil into the hinges of the gates.

Inside the railing was Baba Yaga's hut, and it stood on hen's legs and walked about the yard. And in the yard there was standing Baba Yaga's servant, and she was crying bitterly because of the tasks Baba Yaga set her to do. She was crying bitterly and wiping her eyes on her petticoat.

"How lucky," says the little girl, "that I picked up a handkerchief!" And she gave the handkerchief to Baba Yaga's servant, who wiped her eyes on it and smiled through her tears.

Close by the hut was a huge dog, very thin, gnawing a dry crust.

"How lucky," says the little girl, "that I picked up a loaf!" And she gave the loaf to the dog, and he gobbled it up and licked his lips.

The little girl went bravely up to the hut and knocked on the door.

"Come in," says Baba Yaga.

The little girl went in, and there was Baba Yaga, the bony-legged, the witch, sitting weaving at the loom. In a corner of the hut was a thin black cat watching a mousehole.

"Good day to you, Auntie," says the little girl, trying not to tremble.

"Good day to you, Niece," says Baba Yaga.

"My stepmother has sent me to you to ask for a needle and thread to mend a shirt."

"Very well," says Baba Yaga, smiling and showing her iron teeth. "You sit down here at the loom and go on with my weaving, while I go and get you the needle and thread."

The little girl sat down at the loom and began to weave.

Baba Yaga went out and called to her servant, "Go, make the bath hot and scrub my niece. Scrub her clean. I'll make a dainty meal of her."

The servant came in for the jug. The little girl begged her, "Be not too quick in making the fire, and carry the water in a sieve." The servant smiled, but said nothing, because she was afraid of Baba Yaga. But she took a very long time about getting the bath ready.

Baba Yaga came to the window and asked, "Are you weaving, little niece? Are you weaving, my pretty?"

"I am weaving, Auntie," says the little girl.

When Baba Yaga went away from the window, the little girl spoke to the thin black cat who was watching the mousehole.

"What are you doing, thin black cat?"

"Watching for a mouse," says the thin black cat. "I haven't had any dinner for three days."

"How lucky," says the little girl, "that I picked up the scraps of meat!" And she gave them to the thin black cat.

The thin black cat gobbled them up and said to the little girl, "Little girl, do you want to get out of this?"

"Catkin dear," says the little girl, "I do want to

get out of this, for Baba Yaga is going to eat me with her iron teeth."

"Well," says the cat, "I will help you."

Just then Baba Yaga came to the window.

"Are you weaving, little niece?" she asked. "Are you weaving, my pretty?"

"I am weaving, Auntie," says the little girl, working away, while the loom went clickety-clack, clickety-clack.

Baba Yaga went away.

Says the thin black cat to the little girl, "You have a comb in your hair, and you have a towel. Take them and run for it while Baba Yaga is in the bathhouse. When Baba Yaga chases after you, you must listen; and when she is close to you, throw away the towel, and it will turn into a big, wide river. It will take her a little time to get over that. But when she does, you must listen; and as soon as she is close to you, throw away the comb, and it will sprout up into such a forest that she will never get through it at all."

"But she'll hear the loom stop," says the little girl.

"I'll see to that," says the thin black cat.

The cat took the little girl's place at the loom.

Clickety-clack, clickety-clack — the loom never stopped for a moment.

The little girl looked to see that Baba Yaga was in the bathhouse, and then she jumped down from the little hut on hen's legs and ran to the gates as fast as her legs could carry her.

The big dog leapt up to tear her to pieces. But just as he was going to spring on her, he saw who she was.

"Why, this is the little girl who gave me the loaf," said he. "A good journey to you, little girl," and he lay down again with his head between his paws.

When she came to the gates they opened quietly, quietly, without making any noise at all, because of the oil she had poured into their hinges.

Outside the gates there was a little birch tree that beat her in the face so that she could not go by.

"How lucky," says the little girl, "that I picked up the ribbon!" And she tied up the birch tree with the pretty blue ribbon. And the birch tree was so pleased with the ribbon that it stood still, admiring itself, and let the little girl go by.

How she did run!

Meanwhile the thin black cat sat at the loom. Clickety-clack, clickety-clack, sang the loom, but you never saw such a tangle as the tangle made by the thin black cat.

And presently Baba Yaga came to the window.

"Are you weaving, little niece?" she asked. "Are you weaving, my pretty?"

"I am weaving, Auntie," says the thin black cat, tangling and tangling, while the loom went clickety-clack, clickety-clack.

"That's not the voice of my little dinner," says Baba Yaga, and she jumped into the hut, gnashing her iron teeth; and there was no little girl, but only the thin black cat sitting at the loom, tangling and tangling the threads.

"Grr," says Baba Yaga, and jumps for the cat and begins banging it about. "Why didn't you tear the little girl's eyes out?"

"In all the years I have served you," says the cat, "you have only given me one little bone; but the kind little girl gave me scraps of meat."

Baba Yaga threw the cat into a corner and went out into the yard.

"Why didn't you squeak when she opened you?" she asked the gates.

"Why didn't you tear her to pieces?" she asked the dog.

"Why didn't you beat her in the face, and not let her go by?" she asked the birch tree.

"Why were you so long in getting the bath

ready? If you had been quicker, she never would have got away," said Baba Yaga to the servant.

And she rushed about the yard, beating them all and scolding at the top of her voice.

"Ah!" said the gates, "in all the long years we have served you, you never even eased us with water; but the kind little girl poured good oil into our hinges."

"Ah!" said the dog, "in all the years I've served you, you never threw me anything but burnt crusts; but the kind little girl gave me a good loaf."

"Ah!" said the little birch tree, "in all the years I've served you, you never tied me up, even with thread; but the kind little girl tied me up with a gay blue ribbon."

"Ah!" said the servant, "in all the years I've served you, you have never given me even a rag; but the kind little girl gave me a pretty handker-chief."

Baba Yaga gnashed at them with her iron teeth. Then she jumped into her mortar and sat down. She drove it along with the pestle and swept up her tracks with a broom and flew off in pursuit of the little girl.

The little girl ran and ran. She put her ear to the ground and listened. Bang, bang, bangety bang!

She could hear Baba Yaga beating the mortar with the pestle. Baba Yaga was quite close. There she was, beating with the pestle and sweeping with the broom, coming along the road.

As quickly as she could, the little girl took out the towel and threw it on the ground. And the towel grew bigger and bigger, and wetter and wetter, and there was a deep, broad river between Baba Yaga and the little girl.

The little girl turned and ran on. How she ran!

Baba Yaga came flying up in the mortar. But the mortar could not float in the river with Baba Yaga inside. She drove it in, but only got wet for her trouble. Tongs and pokers tumbling down a chimney are nothing to the noise she made as she gnashed her iron teeth. She turned home and went flying back to the little hut on hen's legs. Then she got together all her cattle and drove them to the river.

"Drink, drink!" she screamed at them, and the cattle drank up all the river to the last drop. And Baba Yaga, sitting in the mortar, drove it with the pestle and swept up her tracks with the broom, and flew over the dry bed of the river and on in pursuit of the little girl.

The little girl put her ear to the ground and

listened. Bang, bang, bangety bang! She could hear Baba Yaga beating the mortar with the pestle. Nearer and nearer came the noise, and there was Baba Yaga, beating with the pestle and sweeping with the broom, coming along the road close behind.

The little girl threw down the comb, and it grew bigger and bigger, and its teeth sprouted up into a thick forest — so thick that not even Baba Yaga could force her way through. And Baba Yaga, gnashing her teeth and screaming with rage and disappointment, turned around and drove away home to her little hut on hen's legs.

The little girl ran on home. She was afraid to go in and see her stepmother, so she ran into the shed.

Scratch, scratch! Out came the little mouse.

"So you got away all right, my dear," says the little mouse. "Now run in. Don't be afraid. Your father is back, and you must tell him all about it."

The little girl went into the house.

"Where have you been?" says her father. "And why are you so out of breath?"

The stepmother turned yellow when she saw her, and her eyes glowed and her teeth ground together until they broke.

But the little girl was not afraid, and she went to her father and climbed on his knee and told him everything just as it had happened. And when the old man knew that the stepmother had sent his little daughter to be eaten by Baba Yaga, he was so angry that he drove her out of the hut, and ever afterward lived alone with the little girl. Much better it was for both of them.

The
Bewitching
Ointment

SQUIRE LOVELL HAD A HOUSEKEEPER who was celebrated for two things. One was her beautiful spin-
ning and weaving, and the other was her curiosity.
Joan was her name, and her prying habits were the
cause of an adventure which landed her in more
trouble than she had bargained for.

It began one Saturday afternoon when the
Squire asked Joan to do some errands for him. Joan
agreed willingly because she always enjoyed a
day in town. The sun was shining out of a blue sky,
birds were singing and insects humming as she
set out, looking forward to the long walk over the
moors.

She had to pass the village where Betty Trenance lived, and she thought how pleasant it would
be to call at Betty's cottage for a cup of tea and
gossip and, most important, to learn what the
neighbors had been up to since her last visit. People said that Betty Trenance was a witch, but Joan
did not mind that. "Witch or no witch," she said
to herself, "any company is better than none, and
I get tired of talking to myself."

When she arrived at Betty's cottage, she did not
knock at the door as a polite visitor would have
done, but stooped down to peep through the key-
hole. She excused herself by thinking that she
would not go in if Betty was busy washing or iron-
ing. What she saw, however, made her eyebrows
shoot up in surprise. Betty had her three children
around her and was rubbing their eyes with a
greenish ointment out of a round box. When she
had finished and the last child had gone into the
inner room, Betty put the box away on a ledge in
the chimney corner and covered it with a piece of
cloth.

"I didn't know there was anything wrong with
the children's eyes," Joan muttered. She knocked
on the door and went in.

Betty was delighted to see Joan and immediately
put the kettle on the fire to make the tea.

"I'd better not have any myself," Betty said. "I've got a touch of the rheumatics, and I must take some of my special medicine. I made it myself from milk, suet, brandy, and rue [that's an herb that grows in the meadow], and it does wonders. Sit ye down, Joan, and make yourself comfortable. I'll just have to fetch my medicine from the other room, and while I'm out I'd better see what the children are up to."

She hobbled out of the room, her stiff black dress rustling round her ankles.

As soon as Betty had gone, Joan went to the chimney corner and took the box of ointment. She pushed her finger into it, sniffed at it, and finding that it smelled of nothing very much, she touched her right eye with the green stuff. She blinked and looked around her.

To her amazement, the whole scene had changed. The room was full of small creatures dancing about, tossing up their heels, waving their feathered caps, swinging on the cobwebs that hung from the rafters, and riding mice in and out through holes in the thatched roof. There were little men dressed in green, wearing high riding boots with silver spurs on their heels. There were little women in gowns of green velvet with long trains. Their high-heeled shoes sparkled with dia-

mond buckles and they all wore high-crowned
steeple hats.

Gaily colored birds flew in and out of the open
window, singing as if their hearts were bursting
with happiness. Then a troop of small people entered through the window playing musical instruments: pipes, flutes, reeds, and shells. Joan
had never heard such entrancing sounds. The
musicians were followed by more men and women,
none over three inches high, all carrying bunches
of herbs and flowers. They formed a half-circle
and stood waiting.

Betty came back into the room. She took no notice of Joan, but sat down on her stool before the
fire and spread her apron over her knees. The little men immediately came forward and began to
cast their herbs and plants in her apron. Then the
women came forward, and they poured over Betty's old dress all the dews and dyes they had gathered from sea and land.

The magic liquids had no sooner touched the
material than it was changed into velvet edged
with silver cord. Little sprigs of flowers appeared
all over the dress, making Betty look lovelier than
any Queen of the May. The air was full of a sweet
summer perfume, and Joan's senses were so over-

come with all she had seen that she hardly knew whether she was awake or asleep.

She blinked her eyes again, and in an instant the little people had vanished. All she could see was the dusty room and Betty, in her old black dress, looking at her strangely.

"Wake up, Joan," she heard the witch say. "The heat must have made you sleepy."

"Yes, I suppose that was it," Joan answered, rubbing her eyes and looking around her.

"You haven't been near that ointment on the ledge, have you?" Betty asked in a sharp voice.

"What — er — what ointment?" Joan stammered.

"Oh, just something for the children's eyes," Betty said. "I make it myself from four-leaf clovers gathered on the night of the full moon."

"Oh yes, of course," Joan said. "It must be very healing."

Betty said no more and got on with making the tea. The two women chatted for a time, and then Joan said, "If I don't hurry, it will be dark before I arrive, and I must get back tonight."

Betty did not seem anxious to keep her. She waved good-bye from the cottage door, then went in and closed the door firmly behind her.

Joan set off in a very thoughtful mood, but by the time she had reached town she decided that she had indeed dropped off to sleep in Betty's cottage and had dreamed of the little people and all they had done. She bought the things she had to get for the Squire, and was ready to set off for home when she saw Betty's husband, Tom Trenance. She was about to call to him, but there was something odd about his behavior, so she hid behind a stall and watched.

Tom Trenance was creeping about in the shadows, openly picking up things from the stalls and putting them into his large pockets. From one stall he took shoes and stockings, from another a hank of yarn, and pewter spoons from a third. There were many people passing to and fro, yet nobody seemed to notice him, but looked straight through Tom as though he were completely invisible.

Joan thought it all very strange, and her curiosity would not allow her to leave things alone. She walked up to Tom and put a hand on his arm.

"Tom," she said sternly, "aren't you ashamed to go round picking up things from one stall after another? And with people all around you too! Aren't you afraid of being caught stealing and taken off to prison?"

Tom looked very surprised at being spoken to. He frowned at Joan and then, without answering her question, said, "Which eye can you see me with?"

Joan shut her left eye. With the other she saw Tom standing in front of her, his pockets bulging, his face angry. Then she closed her right eye, opened her left, and was greatly astonished to see the market place and the crowds passing by, but no sign of Tom.

"Well, Joan," Tom repeated, "which eye is it — right or left?"

"It's very queer," Joan said slowly, "but there seems to be something wrong with my left eye — I can't see you at all!"

"So you see me with your right eye, do you?" Tom said thoughtfully. He hesitated for a moment, then he put one finger on her right eye.

After a moment Joan opened her eye. Not only had Tom vanished, but she found she could not see anything out of it at all. "What's happened?" she asked herself in sudden panic. "Am I dreaming again, or have I been bewitched?" She must get home quickly and tell the Squire what had happened.

Joan left the market place and found the road that led out of town. But she could not keep to it.

She stumbled and lurched, and kept tumbling into the ditch on her blind side. She grew so tired that she could scarcely drag one leg after the other, and so unhappy that she could not help sobbing aloud. Her right eye was hurting her, the basket was heavy, and she wished she had never been born. "Oh," she whimpered, "if only I could find a quiet old horse that would carry me home."

No sooner had the words been uttered than her wish was granted. There, by the roadside, stood an old white horse, bony and feeble, but a horse!

Joan untied the halter, which was fastened to a stunted bush, and placed it over the horse's head. She found a large stone for a mounting block, rolled it up to the horse, and managed to heave herself onto the horse's back. "Take me home, old horse," Joan said wearily.

For a long time the horse would not budge. Joan rattled her heels against its sides and smacked its hindquarters sharply, and at last the animal moved forward at a snail's pace. Joan beat and kicked and coaxed, but the horse would only creep slowly until it got to the top of the hill. Then suddenly it went like the wind!

It tore down the hill, with Joan hanging onto its mane, then left the ground altogether and sailed through the air. Over hedges and ditches the horse flew, over fields and sleeping villages. "Whoa, whoa!" cried Joan until she could shout no longer. But the horse put back its ears and sped ever onward.

At length they came to Toldava Moor. The horse began to slacken speed, and when they were over a large pond it started to dive downward. Joan was certain that it would plunge them both into the water. She gave a shriek, let go of the mane, and threw herself off the brute's back.

Luckily she fell into a bed of soft rushes at the very edge of the pond. Much shaken, she crawled onto firm land and lay there gasping for breath. When she looked up, she saw that what she had been riding was a horse no longer. It seemed as though a blazing ball of fire were streaming through the night, followed by the devil and a pack of headless hounds.

Joan shook her head numbly. She couldn't make out what it was all about, and she was too tired to try. She dragged herself across the rough ground as best she could. Her shoes were lost in the pond and the things had disappeared from her basket.

Ahead of her she saw the outline of a barn, and thankfully crawled toward it. She pushed the door open and fell inside, and was soon fast asleep.

Halfway through Sunday morning she was

awakened by the voice of Squire Lovell. "What have you been up to, my good woman?" she heard him say angrily.

Joan was too miserable to answer. She dragged herself to her feet and stood before him, dirty and bedraggled, her hair matted and her clothes torn.

"What have you been up to?" the Squire repeated. He turned to the two men who were with him. "It's a good thing we came out to round up the sheep," he said, "or I doubt if I should ever have seen this drunken housekeeper of mine again."

Joan tried to pull herself together. "I'm not drunk! It was the fairy ointment that did it."

"Fairy fiddlesticks!" the Squire snorted. "Climb onto my horse and I'll take you home."

Joan shrank back. "I never want to see another horse as long as I live. It was a horse that brought me to the pond and nearly drowned me. Then it turned into a ball of fire."

"First it's ointment, then it's a horse!" the Squire said grimly. "You must have had a night of it. I suppose you went to visit your friend, Betty Trenance?"

"I did call on her," Joan admitted. "That was where I saw all the fairies, and heard their music, and smelled the perfumes they brought — "

The Squire turned to one of his men. "Go and get Doctor Tregear to call at the house as soon as he can," he said. "And I'll get this poor woman home. Next time I want things from the market I'll go myself, and she can stay at home weaving!"

Joan argued no more. She allowed herself to be led out of the barn, put on the horse's back, and taken to the Squire's house. When they got there, she went straight to bed and stayed there for several days.

Gradually the sight came back to her right eye, but she was never the same woman again. Nobody would believe her story, though she insisted till the day she died that her troubles had started when she had investigated the fairy ointment. She never went near the Trenance cottage again, and warned all young girls not to make friends with Betty Trenance.

As for Betty, when she was asked about Joan and the fairy ointment, all she would say with a cackling laugh, was, "Well, curiosity nearly killed *that* cat, didn't it?"

The
Hungry
Old Witch

SHE WAS A WITCH, she was very old, and she was always hungry, and she lived long ago near a forest, just in the corner where Brazil and Argentina touch. Those were the days when mighty beasts moved in the marshes, and when strange creatures with wings like bats flew in the air. There were also great worms then, so strong that they bored through mountains and rocks as an ordinary worm makes its way through clay.

The size and the strength of the old witch may be guessed when you know that she once caught one of the giant worms and killed it for the sake of the stone in its head. And there is this about the stone: it is green in color and shaped like an arrowhead, a little blunted, and precious for those who know the secret, because he who has one may fly through the air between sunrise and sunset, but never in the night.

The old witch had another secret thing. It was a powder, and the knowledge of how to make it was hers alone and is now lost. All that is known of it is that it was made from the fried bodies of tree frogs mixed with goat's milk. With it she could, by sprinkling a little of it where wanted, make things grow wonderfully.

She could also turn plants to animals with it, or change vines into serpents, thornbushes into foxes, little leaves into ants. Living creatures she also changed, turning cats into jaguars, lizards into alligators, and bats into horrible flying things.

This old witch had lived for hundreds of years — so long indeed that the memory of men did not know a time when she was not, and fathers and grandfathers and great-grandfathers all had the same tale to tell of how she had always devoured cattle and pigs and goats, making no account at all of carrying off in one night all the animals of a village.

To be sure some had tried to fight her by shooting arrows; but it was of no use, for by her magic the shafts were bent into a shape like a letter V as soon as they touched her. So in time it came about that men would put outside the village in a corral one half of what they had raised in a year, letting the old witch take it, hoping that thus she would leave them in peace.

At last there grew up a lad, a sober fellow of courage, who said little and thought much, and he refused to take animals to the corral when the time came for the old witch to visit that place.

When the people asked him his reason for refusing, he said that he had had a dream in which he saw himself as a bird in a cage; but when he had been there a little while a sweet climbing vine had grown up about the cage, and on this vine was a white flower which twisted its way in between the bars. Then, as he looked at it, the flower changed to a smiling maiden who held a golden key in her hand. This key she had given to him, and with it he had opened the door of the cage. So, he went on to say, both he and the maiden had gone away.

What the end of the dream was he did not know, for at that point he had wakened with the sound of singing and music in his ears, from which he judged that all turned out well, though he had not seen the end of it.

Because of this dream and what it might betoken he said that he would not put anything in the corral for the old witch, but instead would venture forth and seek her out, to the end that the land might be free from her witcheries and evil work. Nor could anyone persuade him to the contrary.

"It is not right," he said, "that we should give away for nothing that which we have grown and tended and learned to love; nor is it right that we should feed and fatten the evil thing that destroys us."

So the wise men of that place named the lad by a word which means Stout Heart; and because he was loved by all, many trembled and turned pale when the morning came on which he took his lance and alone went off into the forest, ready for whatever might befall him.

For three days Stout Heart walked, and at last came to a place all grassy and flowery, where he sat down by the side of a lake under a tree. He was tired, for he had walked far that day and found

that slumber began to overtake him. That was well
enough, for he was used to sleep under the bare
heavens; but with his slumber came confused
dreams of harmful things which he seemed to see
coming out of the ground, so he climbed into the
tree, where he found a resting place among the
branches and was soon asleep.

While he slept, there came to the side of the lake
the old witch, who cast her basket net into the water and began to fish, and as she fished she sang in
a croaking and harsh voice this song:

> Things in the air,
> Things in the water —
> Nothing is fair,
> So come to the slaughter.

They were not the words, but that is what the
words meant. But unpleasant as was the song, yet
it worked a kind of charm, and things came to her,
so that her basket net was filled again and again.
The fish she cast into a kind of wicker cage, of
which she had several.

Soon the croaking song chased sleep from the
eyes of Stout Heart, and looking down he saw the
wrinkled crone and the great pile of fish that she

had cast on the bank, and his heart was grieved for two things: one that there was such waste of good life, the other that he had left his spear hidden in the grass.

He grieved too, a little, because he knew that on account of his long walk he was weak from hunger and thirst. So there seemed little that could be done, and he sat very still, trusting that until he was better prepared for action the old witch would not see him.

But all his stillness was of no avail. Looking at the shadow of the tree as it lay upon the surface of the water, she saw the lad's image. Then she looked up and saw him. Had she had her magic green stone with her, things would have been far different and this tale all the shorter. But not having it and being quite unable to climb trees, she said:

"You are faint and hungry. Come down, come down, good lad, for I have much here that is good to eat."

Hearing that, Stout Heart laughed, knowing that she was not to be trusted, and he told her that he was very well indeed where he was. So she tried another trick, spreading on the grass fruits and berries, and saying in a wheedling voice:

"Come, son, eat with me. I do not like to eat alone. Here are fresh fruits and here is honey. Come down that I may talk with you and treat you as a son, for I am very lonesome."

But Stout Heart still laughed at her, although to be sure he was a lad of great appetite and his hunger increased in him.

"Have you any other trap to set for me?" he asked.

Hearing that, the old witch fell into a black and terrible rage, dancing about and gnashing her teeth, frothing at the mouth and hooking her long nails at him like a cat, and the sight of her was very horrible, but the lad kept his heart up and was well content with his place in the tree, the more as he saw her great strength.

For in her rage she plucked a great rock the size of a man's body from the earth, where it was sunk deep, and cast it at the tree with such force that the tree shook from root to tip.

For a moment the old witch stood with knit brows, then she went on her hands and knees and fell to gathering up blades of grass until she had a little heap. All the time she was cursing and groaning, grumbling and snarling like a cat. When

she had gathered enough grass, she stood up and
began to sprinkle a grayish powder over the grass
heap, and as she did this she talked mumblingly,
saying:

> Creep and crawl — creep and crawl!
> Up the tree-trunk, on the branch.
> Creep and crawl — creep and crawl!
> Over leaf and over twig.
>
> Seek and find the living thing.
> Pinch him, bite him, torture him.
> Creep and crawl — creep and crawl!
> Make him drop like rotting fruit.

So she went on, moving about in a little circle
and sprinkling the powder over the grass. Presently the pile of grass began to move as if it hid
some living thing, and soon the grass blades became smaller, rounded themselves, and turned
brown. Then from them shot out fine hairlike
points which became legs, and so each separate
leaf turned to an ant.

To the tree they scurried and up the trunk they
swarmed, a little army marching over every leaf
and twig until the green became brown, and louder

and louder the old witch screamed, waving her arms the while:

> Creep and crawl — creep and crawl!
> Up the tree-trunk, on the branch.
> Creep and crawl — creep and crawl!

The nearer to Stout Heart that they came, the louder she shrieked, leaping about and waving her long-taloned hands as she ordered:

> Seek and find the living thing.

Then Stout Heart knew that trouble was brewing indeed, for against so many enemies there was no way to fight. For a time he avoided them, but for a time only, and that by going higher and higher in the tree, crawling along the branch that hung over the lake; but nearer and nearer the ants came, and louder she bade them to

> Pinch him, bite him, torture him.

At last there was nothing for it but to drop out of the tree, for he had been hanging to the end of a branch, and the ants were already swarming over his hands and some running down his arms. So he let go his hold and went into the lake with a plash, down out of the sunshine and into the cool green-blue of the waters. He swam a little, trying to get out of the way before coming up, but had to put his head out soon to get a breath of air.

Then suddenly he seemed to be in the middle of something that was moving about strangely, and it was with a sudden leaping of the heart that he found himself in the old witch's basket net, being drawn ashore. To be sure he struggled and tried to escape, but it was of no use. What with her magic and her strength he was no more in her hands than is a little fish in the hands of a man.

He was all mixed up with other lake things — with fish and with scum, with water beetles and sticky weed, with mud and with wriggling creatures — and presently he found himself toppled head foremost into a basket, all dazed and weak. It was dark there, but by the bumping he knew that he was being carried somewhere.

Soon he was tumbled into an evil-smelling place, and must have fallen into a trance or slept. Again, he may not have known what passed because of the old witch's enchantments, for when he came to himself he did not know whether he had been there for a long time or a little.

But soon he made out that he was in a stone house and, through a small hole in the wall, saw that the place where the house stood was bare of grass and full of great gray rocks, and he remembered his dream and thought that it was all very unlike what had really happened.

But in that he was not altogether right, for while he was in no cage and no twining vine with glorious flower there, yet there was something else. For after a little while a door opened, and he saw standing in a light that nearly blinded him with its brightness a maiden full of winning grace, light and slender, who stretched out her hand to him and led him out of the dark into a great hall of stone with a vast fireplace. Then having heard his story, which brought tears to her blue eyes, she opened a lattice and showed him a little room where he might hide.

"For," said she, "I also was brought to this place long ago, and when I came the old witch killed the one who was her slave before me. But before she died she told me the story of the green stone which the witch has, and also how the magic powders were used.

"Since then I have been here alone and have been her slave. But now she will kill me and will keep you for her servant until she tires of you, when she will catch another. And so it has been for many, many years, and each one that dies has told the power of the green stone to the other, though none had dared to use it."

Now hearing all that, Stout Heart was all for running away at once and taking the maiden from that dreadful place, but just as he opened his mouth to speak there came to their ears the voice of the old witch.

"Hide then," said the maiden, "and all may yet go well. For I must go to get the green stone by means of which we may fly. With you I will dare. Alone I was afraid to venture."

Even then he hesitated and did not wish to hide, but she thrust him into a little room and closed the door. Through the wall he heard the old witch enter and throw a pile of wood on the hearth.

"I have a new prize," said the ogress. "You I have fattened long enough, and now you must be my meal. One slave at a time is enough for me, and the lad will do. Go then, fetch salt and pepper — both red pepper and black, and see to it that you lose no time, for I am hungry and cannot wait."

The girl went into another room, and the old witch fell on her knees and began to build a roaring fire. Soon the maiden re-entered, but running lightly, and as she passed the old woman she cast on her some of the magic powder which she had brought instead of salt and pepper.

The hag had no idea that it was the powder that the girl had thrown, and thinking that she had been careless with the salt and pepper began to scold her; then getting to her feet she took her by the hair, opened the door of the little room in which Stout Heart was, and, little knowing that the lad was there, cast her in, screaming:

"Stay there, useless one, until I am ready to roast you!"

The maiden thrust the green stone into the hands of Stout Heart, and at once they flew through the window and out under the arch of the sky. As for the old witch, the powder did its work, and she began to swell so that she could not pass out of any of the doors. But presently the boy and girl, from a height at which they could see below them the narrow valley and the witch house, saw that the old hag was struggling to get out by way of the roof.

The two lost no time then. They flew swift and high. But swift too was the old witch. Her growing had finished, and out over the top of the house she burst and, seeing the escaping pair, began to run in the direction they had taken.

So there was much speeding both in the air and on the earth, and unlucky it was for the two that the green stone allowed those who carried it to fly only in the daytime. All this the maiden told Stout Heart as they flew. The old witch well remembered that at night there was no power in the flying stone, and was gleeful in her wicked old heart as she watched the sun and the lengthening shadows.

So she kept on with giant strides and leapings, and going at such a rate that she was always very nigh under the two in the air. No deer, no huanaco could have bounded lighter over the ground than she did, and no ostrich could have moved swifter.

When the sun began to drop in the western sky, and the two were looking at each other with concern as they flew, the maiden bethought her of a plan, and scattering some of the magic powder on the earth she rejoiced to see that the leaves on which the powder fell turned into rabbits. The sight of that the old witch could not resist, and she stopped a moment to catch some of the little animals and swallow them, so a little time was won for the fliers.

But the hungry old witch soon went on, and regained the time she had lost and was under them again, running as fast as ever. So more powder was scattered, this time on some thornbushes, which changed to foxes. Again the old woman stopped to eat, and the two gained a little. But the sun was lower, and they found themselves dropping ever nearer to the earth, flying indeed but little higher than the treetops; and they could see the old witch, in her leaps, was almost touching them.

Ahead of them was the lake in which Stout Heart had been caught, the waters red as blood with the light of the western sky, but the power of the stone was failing with the waning day, and of the powder they had but a small handful left. As for the old witch, so near was she that they could hear her breathing, could almost imagine that they felt her terrible claws in their garments.

On the bank of the lake they cast the last handful of the magic powder, and they saw the grass turn to ants and the stones to great turtles as they passed over the water, but so low were they now that their feet almost touched the surface of the lake. The power of the stone was growing steadily weaker.

The old witch, seeing the turtles, stopped to swallow them, shells and heads, and that gave the youth and maiden time enough to reach the opposite shore, where the power of the stone was quite exhausted as the sun touched the rim of the earth.

The gentle maiden clung to Stout Heart in great fear then as they saw the old witch plunge into the lake, for she could travel on water as fast as she could on land. Indeed, the fearful old hag cut through the waters so swiftly that a great wave leaped up on each side of her, and it was clear that before the sun had gone she would have her claws in the two friends.

But when she was in the middle of the lake the weight of the turtles she had swallowed began to bear her down. In vain she struggled, making a great uproar and lashing her hands and feet so furiously that the water became hot and a great steam rose up. Her force was spent, and the turtles were like great stones within her, so she sank beneath the water and was seen no more.

Great was the joy of the people when Stout Heart brought the maiden to his home, for she became his wife and was loved by all there as the fairest woman among them.

The
Young
Witch-Horse

THERE LIVED A YOUNG FARMER in New Jersey — his name was James — who was as handsome as could be. He was tall and had brown eyes, his hair was curly, and he had winning ways. And he had plenty of courage besides.

Now James loved horses more than anything else. Horses to ride and horses to walk, horses to race and horses to pet. He had plenty of them in his stalls, and he took as good care of them as he did of himself. He combed them and curried them and saw that they were shod.

The blacksmith, a fine fellow, had the prettiest wife in town. She had black eyes and black hair, and folks said there was gypsy blood in her veins. Soon James and the blacksmith and his wife were very good friends.

James was there evenings, and they would all talk of this and that, but mostly of the strange goings on in the valley. There were witches at work!

Animals turned sick; young children were ailing, and no doctoring could help; often all the churning would not turn cream into butter.

Folks were scared and watched warily.

James and the blacksmith and his beautiful gypsy-looking wife spoke about it one night, but she only laughed and cried, "What if there are witches hereabouts? They don't do half the harm that's done by good folks."

"That's not true, and you know it well," James said warmly. "I don't like witches, and we should treat 'em as they do in Salem in New England."

But the blacksmith did not believe in hanging people. His pretty young wife laughed, showing her straight white teeth and said, "James, maybe if you meet a handsome witch you'll think differently."

She looked at him with her jet-black eyes until

he felt that she was looking right through him.

James went home thinking of witches and the blacksmith's wife. He felt queerer than he'd ever felt before; the cries of the whippoorwills and katydids had a strange sound in the white night.

He passed by a bog and looked into the water. A pair of black eyes looked at him . . . and the bullfrogs were booming croaking laughter!

"I am bewitched," he said, and tried to keep his head clear.

He went to sleep and slept right well, forgetting his silly thoughts. But at midnight he was awakened by a woman's mocking laughter.

A woman's hand held his, and he was whisked out of his bed into the open under the white moon. They flew on till they came to a wide green, where he saw shadowy creatures and heard the scraping of a fiddle. On a black pine stump sat a tall man, a dark cloak covering all of him save his head, which had two little horns on it.

James knew at once it was the devil, but he did not know who the shadowy girl was who'd brought him through the air. She had on a cloak that covered her all over, and only now and then he saw two jet-black eyes which he thought he had seen before.

The creatures on the green began swirling to the tune of the violin, and the girl who'd brought him began whirling with James the same as the others. Try as he would, he could not stop. On and around they went, with never a rest.

Suddenly there was the crowing of a cock, and whisht! his black-eyed partner rushed him through the air and he was home, tired and worn out.

He slept but little that night, or for many a night thereafter. Every midnight the young, black-eyed witch came and whisked him off to the green to dance.

She never spoke to him; nor did the others. Just danced, nothing else. He never saw her either, only her coal-black eyes.

Often he cried that he did not want to go. Then she'd laugh, and a familiar voice would say, "It's fun to dance with a nice young man!" and whisk him through the air.

Folks noticed how wan and worn James looked.

One day when he was in the tavern he told his closest friend what happened every night. The fellow knew all about witches, so he said:

"The next time the witch comes to take you to her Sabbath dance, take along a halter. When you see your chance, bridle her with it, and then you'll be master over her, and she will do your bidding instead of you hers."

The next night James lay down to sleep in his coat with a halter hidden under it. No sooner did the witch get hold of his hand, and they were out and up in the air, than he threw the halter over her.

Then the strangest thing in all the world happened. When the halter was on her neck the witch . . . turned into a fine black steed!

James was puzzled, as anyone would be, but loving horseflesh and feeling the fine horse under him, he rode her through the moonlit roads and then into the stable.

First thing the next morning James went into the stable to see the new horse. There it stood, a fine coal-black mare with silky mane, but he noticed she was unshod.

He took her at once to his friend the blacksmith.

The blacksmith brought out some iron horseshoes and put them in the fire. When the fire was glowing red he took one with his pliers, went up to the mare, and raised her front hoof and put the red-hot shoe to it. But no sooner did the sizzling metal touch the hoof than there was a great flame in the smithy, the room filled with smoke that had a strange odor, and there before them was no horse . . . but the blacksmith's black-eyed wife, with a fresh burn on her hand! Her eyes were flashing fury.

She ran out screaming, and the blacksmith roared for her never to come back.

She never did come back, and James was never plagued by witches again.

The Witch of Wandaland

KING PAUL RULED OVER A COUNTRY that had no name. It was not a big country, but it was very beautiful. The warm brown rocks of the coastline led to yellow beaches, where the turquoise sea lapped gently at high tide and the breakers burst into sparkling white foam.

Inland the corn grew fat in the summer sunshine. Sturdy sheep and sleek cattle grazed in lush meadows. The trees were tall and straight, the flowers brilliant in color, the lakes cool and clear, and the people kind and peace-loving. No warriors ever came to conquer this land with no name;

there were no tourists to tour, no planners to plan.

King Paul had one daughter, the Princess May, whom he loved dearly. She was very beautiful, with golden hair and laughing blue eyes. Although she was a princess to her fingertips, May was happiest when she was working with the farmers, helping them to sow corn, gather in the harvest, and look after the farm animals. No job was too long, difficult, or dirty for her. With her sleeves rolled up and her hair tied back with a blue ribbon, she was to be found in the fields or the barns more often than in the palace.

One day, when King Paul was sitting on his throne, he found himself sighing deeply.

"Why, I'm unhappy!" he exclaimed to himself. "That's very odd. I have my beautiful country, my lovely daughter, and my loyal people — everything a king could wish for. And yet — " He sighed again and glanced at the empty throne next to his — "I am unhappy. I wonder why?"

At that moment the Prime Minister entered the throne room with a document to be signed. He noticed how sad the King was looking, and ventured to ask if there was anything he could do to help. King Paul told the old man that he was unhappy and asked him if he could think of a reason.

The Prime Minister nodded gravely. "If I may suggest, Your Majesty, your problem is quite a simple one. For eighteen years you have had no queen — not since Queen Margaret died when Princess May was born. Now it has suddenly come home to you that you are lonely. The burdens of kingship are difficult to bear without a helpmate."

The King scratched his chin. "I think you are right," he said. "I do need a queen to grace this noble throne, to wear the royal diadem, to play dominoes with me — and," he added hastily, "to help me bear the burdens of kingship. After all, I can't expect the Princess to sit indoors playing dominoes. She is young and fond of outdoor life. But where can I find a queen, Prime Minister? I could not marry one of my subjects — they are all commoners."

"You will have to travel abroad, Your Majesty," said the Prime Minister. "There are many ladies of royal blood who would willingly be your queen. You will have no difficulty finding one, I assure you."

"One who is willing to be the queen of a country without a name?" the King asked.

"Certainly, Your Majesty," the Prime Minister said proudly. "We may not have a name, but we have riches and contentment, an excellent palace, well-lit streets, and, if I may say so, an extremely handsome monarch."

"Thank you, thank you," said the King. (He was flattered, and made a mental note to award the Prime Minister the Unnamed Order of the Unknown.) "I will set sail tomorrow in search of a queen."

The next day King Paul waved to the crowds who had gathered on the quay to see him off. He felt a pang of sadness as his ship slowly moved away through the sparkling waters of the harbor. The King dabbed at his eyes, cleared his throat, then bravely turned to face the open sea with its promise of strange, exciting lands, in one of which, he hoped, he would find the lady who would be his queen. . . .

A year and a day passed, and King Paul's ship was seen again, at first no bigger than a speck on the horizon. Word that the King was back spread through the town, and all his loyal subjects hurried to the quay again. The Prime Minister summoned the Palace Band. The players hurriedly picked up their instruments and ran, wishing they had had time to practice the National Anthem.

The Royal Cleaners got busy with their mops and dusters, and Princess May left the bran mash she was mixing for the chickens and hastened to the quay.

As the ship drew nearer, the excitement was intense. Whistles blew, bells rang, and flags waved in every direction. When King Paul appeared on deck, the cheers swelled to a roar. He waved; then, almost nervously, he beckoned to a figure in the background to come and stand by his side.

A great sighing gasp arose from the people on the quay, and the cheering rapidly thinned into complete silence. Even the wheeling sea birds stopped screeching, and a gray cloud wiped the brightness from the sky.

The King's voice broke the uncanny silence. "My dear and loyal subjects," he called, "I am happy to present to you your new queen — Queen Wanda." He was about to say more, but stopped suddenly. His loyal subjects had turned their backs on him and were hurrying away from the quay, shaking their heads and muttering fiercely. In a few moments only Princess May remained. Her face had become ashen, and her lips were trembling. "Father," she whispered, "Oh, dear Father, what have you done?"

Queen Wanda stood on deck watching the crowds melt away. She was taller than King Paul, and her raven hair fell to her waist. Her dress was of black velvet, and bloodstones and diamonds flashed from her necklace and bracelets. Her face was ivory-white, her eyes black and cold as a bottomless pool, her lips a streak of cruel vermilion. She smiled at Princess May, and the girl shivered as though the fingers of winter had suddenly clutched at her heart. She knew what the people had seen and what the King, in his innocence, did not know: that her new stepmother was a witch!

During the weeks that followed, King Paul was delighted to find that he was not lonely any more. He asked Queen Wanda's advice on all affairs of state, and would not sign anything without her approval. He was able to play as many games of dominoes as he wished, and noticed nothing of the shadow that had fallen over his once happy country.

The Prime Minister grew more and more concerned about the way things were going, but he was too frightened of the Queen to make any protest. The people hated her, and she hated them back. Princess May, who had been brought up to hate nobody, tried to ignore the fact that the

Queen was bitterly jealous of her and seized every opportunity to make her feel unwanted.

"It's a funny thing," the King said one day, "I never seem to see any of my subjects these days. Wherever we go, there's nobody there!" He and the Queen had just arrived at a state banquet, only to find the great hall almost deserted. Footmen in powdered wigs and full livery stood behind the chairs, but the chairs were empty. "I expect they're very busy," he continued mildly. "After all, it's the height of the harvest season."

"That is not the reason," the Queen said coldly. "Our subjects are both lazy and rebellious, and they must be taught a lesson."

"But, my dear — " the King began to protest.

"Not in front of the servants!" The Queen waved her hand imperiously, and the footmen filed out of the hall. Then she turned to the King. "Paul, look at me!" she commanded.

"Eh, what's that, my dear?" the King asked. He felt his eyes drawn to the Queen's, and hers seemed to bore right into his head and burn into his brain.

She repeated, "They are lazy and rebellious."

The King, dazed, drew a hand over his eyes. "They — they are lazy . . ." he muttered.

"And rebellious," prompted the Queen.

"And rebellious . . ." The King felt words forming on his lips that he could not hold back. "Let's throw them into prison . . ." Then for a moment his mind cleared. "Except that we don't have any prisons!"

"Then we must build one," said the Queen.

The cloud over the King's mind returned. "Yes, we must build one," he agreed tonelessly.

"And while we are making changes, it is high time this country had a name," said the Queen, her eyes glinting with triumph. "My friends cannot write to me because they don't know where to send their letters, and I feel quite cut off. In future the country will be called Wandaland."

"Wandaland," the King repeated. "The country will be called Wandaland." And Wandaland it was, much to everyone's disgust.

The rumor that a prison was to be built spread through the land. No one at first believed their once kind and popular King could be so cruel. Disbelief very soon turned to fear when a forbidding gray building began to rise on the edge of the town. Other things changed, too. No longer did the King hold a daily audience with the Prime Minister. No longer were Fridays set aside for the hearing of grievances. The King rarely ventured outside the palace, and he refused to attend the annual production of the Operatic Society or the Flower

Show. Those who wished to see him had to fill in so many forms that they usually gave up halfway through. Wandaland became a miserable place. The Wandalians (as the Queen insisted they should be called) lost heart. They felt no joy in working hard, so that fields and gardens remained uncultivated, and animals untended. The prison, which was surrounded by a twenty-foot-high wall topped by vicious spikes, dominated the country-side. People began to disappear from their homes in the dead of night. Anguished cries were heard from behind the prison walls, and heartbroken relatives could only guess at the fate of the victims.

At last the Prime Minister, who lived in daily fear of his life, led a group of townspeople to Princess May. The Princess had continued to work on the farm. She saw as little as she could of the Queen, and very little of her father too, since the Queen never left the King's side.

The townspeople found the Princess in the barn. They sat on bundles of hay while the Prime Minister talked. He told the Princess of the many evil things that Queen Wanda had done, and read out a list of the citizens who had disappeared behind the walls of the prison. He told her about the new laws that were making their lives miserable, and described the huge, brutal soldiers who seemed to have appeared from nowhere to form the Queen's private army.

"But worst of all, Your Highness," he said sadly, "the Queen is using vile witchcraft to get your father in her power. She has captured his heart, and is out to ensnare his will. The end of our beautiful country is in sight, and our way of life will be destroyed forever."

The Princess was shocked, and reproached herself for letting such things happen without trying to prevent them. Tears trickled down her cheeks. "What can I do?" she cried. "Is it too late for me to help? Tell me, for I am so ashamed that I have allowed our country to come to such a pass."

"If only you could rescue your father from the Queen's power," said the Prime Minister, and the others nodded in agreement. "If you could get him to realize how wicked she is, that would be the first step toward better things."

The Princess wiped her eyes. Her sadness gave way to determination. "I will do it!" she declared. "This very night I will speak to my father and try to make him understand what is happening. Do not despair. We will outwit Queen Wanda yet!"

That night Princess May made her way boldly to the throne room, determined to say what was in her mind. She knocked loudly on the doors and marched in. "Father — " she began, then stopped when she saw the room was empty, except for the ugly, cross-eyed parrot that was Queen Wanda's special pet.

"Off with you! Off with you!" it squawked raucously. The Princess pulled a face at the bird and hurried out.

She tried the royal bedchamber, but that too was deserted. So were the library, the banquet hall, and the state drawing room. "Surely they can't be in the kitchens," she muttered, "but I'd better go and see." She hurried down passages and round corners, up steps and down steps, and finally came to the kitchens.

Next to the main kitchen was the entrance to the dungeon. The Princess noticed that the iron gate which guarded it was open — something she had never seen before. There was a burly guard at the end of the corridor, with his back to her, tearing at a roasted chicken and flirting with a giggling cook. "Thank goodness his greed has caused him to desert his post," the Princess thought, and slipped through the gate and began cautiously to descend the narrow twisting steps.

As far back as memory could stretch, the dungeon had not been used. There was hardly any light in it, but the Princess could just see the dank, mossy walls, and she heard the scuttering of mice ahead. At the bottom of the steps was a wooden door. She turned the handle — and felt the blood drain from her cheeks.

The dungeon was lit by a luminous green smoke. Her father was cowering against the far wall, terror shining from his eyes. In front of him the Queen leaned over a crucible, from which the green smoke rose in swirling wreaths. Seven small vessels were set in a semicircle before her, and over them she was making writhing gestures with her hands and uttering strange words in a weird droning tone.

The Princess wanted to turn and flee, but the sight of her father enmeshed in the Queen's spell prevented her. With a cry she hurled herself forward, with the intention of somehow destroying the witch's craft.

At the sound of Princess May's voice, the Queen swung round. Her eyes blazed with anger. She thrust her arms forward and screamed out a single word so menacing that the air seemed to quiver with its echo. The Princess stopped abruptly, swayed, then sank down on to the cold stone floor.

The Queen stood over the still figure. Her long fingers, with nails pointed like thorns, curved into grotesque patterns as she feverishly uttered a stream of magic words, and the helpless King was forced to watch a terrible transformation. Slowly his lovely daughter changed into a long, scaly, snakelike creature with the head of a dragon.

Emptied of all human feelings, King Paul begged, "Send it away, my dear, please send it away. . . ."

The Queen lowered her arms and smiled at her husband. "Certainly I will send it away — forever!" she said, and began another incantation. The dragon squirmed to the open door, slithered up the steps, and passed out of their sight.

News of the Princess' disappearance soon flashed through the land. What had happened to her was a mystery, but it was rumored that she had been locked up in the smallest cell of the new prison.

"We shall never see her again, I fear," sighed the Prime Minister to the group of rebels who had gathered with him in the cellars beneath the Town Hall. "She will die in that loathsome place, away from the fields and farms she loved. Our cause is lost!"

He was interrupted by a hammering at the door and a frantic shouting. "Help, help! My farmhouse is on fire!"

" 'Tis Farmer Midwinter," said one of the rebels. "Open the door to him."

The stout, red-faced farmer dashed into the cellar. "A terrible curse is upon us!" he gasped. "A worm — a great ugly creature with a head as fearsome as twenty devils and a tongue of flames — spat fire at my barn and my house, and sent them up in flames! Then it gobbled up two cows and a pig! Come quickly, before everything I own is turned to cinders! Man the pumps, fill the buckets!"

No sooner had Farmer Midwinter blurted out his news than two more frightened men pounded on the door and poured out similar stories of fire and destruction. When the rebels hurried out to see what could be done, they found the townspeople in a state of panic, and confusion everywhere. Men were rushing about, women and children were huddled behind closed doors. Fires ringed the town and lit up the sky with a lurid glare.

"It's the worm — the worm with the dragon's head," people moaned.

During the days that followed, they were forced to watch, helpless, while the scaly monster attacked crops, animals, and buildings. No one could slay it, for no one could get near its fiery breath. Even the ships in the harbor were reduced to ashes, so that there was no way of getting help from neighboring countries.

Just when everything seemed hopeless, the Prime Minister had an idea. "Why didn't I think of it before?" he thought to himself. "The only way to fight the Queen's magic is with more magic — stronger and better magic! I must go and see the Wise Man of the Mountain at once. It is our last chance."

Without telling anyone of his intentions, he set off to climb the highest mountain in the most distant part of the country, where the Wise Man lived in a wooden hut. As the Prime Minister puffed his way up the winding, rock-strewn path, he understood why few people ever bothered to visit the Wise Man. At last, however, he saw the hut through the wispy mountain mist. The Prime Minister staggered the last few yards and rapped at the door.

The Wise Man, his leathery face framed by a long beard and a shock of silver hair, greeted the Prime Minister with a beaming smile. "Good gracious me, a visitor!" he said. "Why, I haven't had a visitor for eight years, three months, and a day, and then it was only someone lost in the fog. Do come in and have a mug of heather tea."

The hut was bare, but bright as a new pin, and

a log fire crackling in the hearth made it warm and cosy. The old man put a huge copper kettle on the fire and busied himself with a tea caddy and spoon. "Is this a social call, or do you want something?" he enquired with a chuckle.

The Prime Minister, out of breath from his climb, could only manage to gasp, "I — want — something."

"A recipe perhaps?" said the Wise Man, getting out two mugs and a teapot. "I have an excellent one for honeysweet moss pudding — delicious!"

"No!" The Prime Minister found his voice. "I want you to help us to kill the ugly worm that is destroying our country at the command of Queen Wanda."

"Wanda!" The Wise Man nearly dropped the kettle as he took it from the fire. "I knew her mother, Gronda — a dreadful old hag with the nastiest line of witchcraft it's ever been my misfortune to be hexed by. What has Wanda been up to?"

Between sips of heather tea, the Prime Minister told his story. When he had finished, the Wise Man shook his head grimly. "You're a bit late, I'm afraid. Still, I'll do my best." He took a pointed wizard's cap from a cupboard and put it on. "By the way," he added casually, "the Princess is not in prison, you know."

"Not?" said the Prime Minister. "Then where — what?"

"She is the worm," said the Wise Man. "That's an old trick of witches, turning a beautiful maiden into an ugly creature."

"Princess May, the worm!" the Prime Minister gasped. "I can't believe it. Why, she loved her people — she wouldn't hurt any of them. As for destroying farms and fields — "

The Wise Man interrupted him. "Not her fault, poor child. It's Wanda's doing. That particular spell runs in her family. Gronda was always turning people into dragons. She tried it on me once, but fortunately I had a portable pentagon in my pocket, and she failed."

"Can't the Princess be turned back again?" the Prime Minister asked.

"That's the trouble with this kind of spell," the Wise Man answered. "A kiss on the head from a prince would do the trick, but what self-respecting prince would kiss a wormy dragon? However, we'll deal with that problem later. First we must reduce some of the fire hazard by stopping the winds." He took up a cord with three knots in it, stood in the middle of the room, and began to chant.

As he untied the first knot, he said, "Gentle

zephyr, wisp of wind, blow your kindly breath upon me. . . ." He untied the second knot, saying, "Brisker wind that fills the sail, whip the strong grass around me. . . ." He untied the third knot, saying, "Tempest fierce, lashing the sea, unleash your mighty storm near me. . . ."

Outside, the Prime Minister could hear three winds. It was most extraordinary. One of them was only a zephyr, one was a howling gale that made the door rattle and the fire flicker, and the third was a raging tempest under which the hut shook and strained — yet he could hear each one separately.

The Wise Man was delighted. He jumped up and down, shouting excitedly, "Good! They're all here now. Excuse me, I must go and have a word with them."

He battled his way through the door, which seemed to resist him with the force of twenty giants, and the Prime Minister heard his voice through the roaring of the winds.

Suddenly all noise stopped, and the shuddering hut became steady. Bright sunshine flooded in as the Wise Man returned. "Well, that's that," he said gleefully. "I've sent a message to the Lord of the Winds. All we can do now is wait and see what happens. Would you like another cup of tea?"

The Prime Minister nodded in bewilderment.

Far beyond the tallest mountain, higher than the highest cloud, was the Land of the Four Winds. There the Lord of the Winds pored over the charts of the journeys made by his messengers. Day and night he sent them forth, the busy trade winds, freezing northerners, wild westerners, warm southerners, and eastern winds with spicy breath. And when they were summoned on special occasions, by the whistling of becalmed sailors or the Wise Man's white witchcraft, the Lord of the Winds was quick to give his help.

Now the Lord of the Winds went into action. He forbade any of his winds to go near Wandaland, so that the fires created from the worm's breath would not spread. Then he ordered them to search far and wide for any rain clouds with nothing special to do, and blow them over the land to extinguish the fires with their rain. Finally he sent for Boreas, one of his four sons — a handsome young man, who fortunately was also brave and strong — and commanded him to set sail immediately for Wandaland, slay the worm, and send the witch-queen packing.

Boreas, always eager for adventure, was delighted to do this. He prepared to set sail, first taking care to fix a branch of the rowan tree to the ship's mast and to wear a necklace of rowanberries to protect him from witchcraft. With a puff from the zephyr, a strong blow from the gale, and a mighty blast from the tempest, the ship took off for Wandaland.

The strange ship appeared on the horizon just as the worm-dragon was heard rumbling on the outskirts of the town. Few people ventured out of doors, but those who did saw the vessel and felt a new lightness of heart. Was this someone coming to save them? they wondered.

But hope vanished when Queen Wanda herself arrived at the quay with a bodyguard of six soldiers. She faced the approaching ship and raised her arms. She began to cast her spell, calling out magic words and making mysterious motions with her hands.

Nothing happened. The ship remained a ship, its well-filled sails carrying it forward strongly. The more the Queen worked her magic, the more resolute seemed the ship's advance. At last she realized that her spell had failed. Letting her arms fall in a gesture of despair, she wheeled around and left the quay in a rage.

Not far away, the worm had slithered into town. The Queen hastened toward it, shrieking, "Sink the ship! Burn it! Hurry, I say!" Then she turned to the soldiers. "Back to the palace — I have work to do."

Boreas felt a pang of horror as the worm crawled nearer. But he was not afraid. He lifted his sword and leaped from the deck onto the quay just as the worm reached it. It spat a long tongue of flame at him; but before the fire touched him, a powerful gust of wind blew it back over the worm's head. Boreas made to strike the beast with his sword. The bright blade was just about to come down when he heard a small, soft voice. It seemed to come from the worm! The sword wavered. Then the voice came again, and this time he heard the words, "Do not strike me, I beg you. Do not strike!"

"It's a trick!" the young man cried. "It's the Queen's magic at work!" And he lifted his sword again.

"Please, please do not kill me," the worm pleaded.

Then another voice was heard, "Don't kill it! Put up your sword!" The Prime Minister was rushing toward them. He clasped the young man's arm. "Kiss it!" he commanded. "Kiss the worm!"

"Kiss that?" cried Boreas, looking with disgust at the writhing creature.

"You are a prince, aren't you?" the Prime Minister asked.

"Yes, of course. My father is the ruler of the winds, so I *must* be. But — "

The Prime Minister fell on his knees. "Then kiss the worm and all will be well, I promise you. There's no time to explain — just do as I say."

Boreas stepped forward hesitantly. The worm lay quite still at his feet. He stooped down and kissed it once, twice, three times on its ugly, scaly head. . . .

Straightaway the worm shuddered and shivered and shrank. The scales fell away. The body dissolved in a mist, and a girl with blue eyes and golden hair emerged.

The Prime Minister clasped his hands in gratitude. "Your Highness," he cried, "welcome back!" He got to his feet shakily, gazing lovingly at the bewildered girl. Then he turned to Boreas. "Young man, may I introduce our dearly beloved Princess May!"

The Princess and Boreas looked at each other with growing interest, while the Prime Minister told them all that had happened since the Princess had "disappeared." Princess May was very distressed. "Did I really do all those horrible things?" she said. "All I can remember is a terrible nightmare from which I could not awake."

"Do not blame yourself, Your Highness," said the Prime Minister. "Everything that happened was the Queen's doing."

"Then she shall pay for her wickedness!" cried Boreas in ringing tones. "Lead me to the palace and I will avenge you all!"

In spite of the Prime Minister's warnings and the Princess' entreaties, Boreas would not be dissuaded. "I must fulfill my task," he said. "The Queen may think she is all-powerful, but do not forget who my father is. Show me the way!"

The six guards at the palace gates roared with laughter at the sight of the young man coming toward them armed only with a sword. They lowered their wicked-looking halberds and pointed them at him. "Come closer, sonny," one of them shouted, "and we will make mincemeat of you!"

The Princess and the Prime Minister, and the crowd which had collected behind them, waited in frightened silence. Then — out of nowhere — came a wind, which grew in strength as Boreas advanced. Not a hair of his head was disarranged, not a ripple disturbed his cloak, but the guards were suddenly struck by a tremendous force. They tried to lunge forward with their halberds, but found themselves rooted to the spot. The weapons flew from their hands, their helmets tumbled from their heads, their clothes flapped around their faces and blinded them, and finally all six fell to the ground and were blown away. Over and over they rolled, until they reached the sea wall and disappeared over the edge.

Then the Princess and Boreas pressed forward to the main doors of the palace, which had been locked and bolted against intruders. With a mighty puff, the wind banged the doors open, and the young couple hurried through the corridors until they reached the iron gate of the dungeon. The guard drew out a dagger as they approached. "Stay where you are — " he began. Then a look of utter astonishment puckered his face as he found himself hurtling down the corridor, through a window, and into a lake in the garden outside.

The Princess and Boreas flew down the stone steps and into the dungeon. In the middle of the floor stood the Queen with King Paul, who was bound to a post with ropes, his kingly robes all torn and dusty.

"Father!" cried the Princess.

"Stop!" the Queen spat out. "If you come any nearer, you will never see your father again. I will

turn him into a toad! You may think you have out-
witted me, but there is no magic known to our
young hero that can stop me!"

The Princess began to wring her hands. "She is
right! She is too clever for us."

By her side she felt Boreas shaking with anger.
"Is that so?" he demanded. "We have not finished
with you yet, Queen Wanda! Evil shall not conquer! Father, Lord of the Winds, come to our aid
once more!"

The Queen grabbed her book of spells as the
wind began to blow. "A toad he shall be!" she
shrieked, and started to gabble the words of a spell.
But before she had finished the first sentence, the
book was blown from her hands and slid across the
floor. The Queen, darting after it, was forced back
against the wall and pinned there, unable to move.
She struggled frantically, her black hair swirling
around her; but the more she fought, the fiercer
became the force that bound her.

"Quick!" shouted Boreas. "Get the book, Princess, and find the spell."

"Don't you dare — " the Queen began, then
choked as though a hand had been clapped over
her mouth. She gurgled into silence.

"Tansy," murmured the Princess, turning over
the pages rapidly. "Tantalus, Tarantula, Termagant,

Termite, Tiddlywinks — ah, here it is — Toad . . ."

"Read it!" said Boreas.

As the Princess read out the spell, the Queen, still held captive by the wind, began to tremble with fear. When the spell was finished, there was an eerie silence in the dungeon. The wind had gone, its work done. The Princess raised her eyes from the book. Instead of the glittering, imperious figure of the witch, she saw a fat brown, warty toad squatting on the floor, croaking faintly.

Princess May shuddered, and for a moment felt guilty at what she had done. Boreas gently released the fainting King, and he and the Princess led him out of the dungeon. As he shot the bolt on the door, the clang echoed through the darkness.

"Let her stay there forever," Boreas said. "She will have time to think on the evil she has done to so many good and innocent people. Come, let us leave this evil dungeon."

The people of the country that had no name — for such it immediately became again — soon forgave the King for his folly, and within a short time the horror of Queen Wanda's rule was only an unhappy memory.

Princess May married the son of the Lord of the Winds and spent half the year in the Lord's domain and half with her father, though much of that time was passed on the farm, where she was still a welcome helper.

The Wise Man of the Mountain gave up being a hermit. He was given a splendid house in the city and was appointed Adviser in Wisdom to All Who Wish to be Wise.

The prison was knocked down and a pleasure garden was built on the site. The prisoners were all awarded a medal for bravery and given a purse full of gold. Everyone in the country that had no name was happy — except the toad croaking dismally in the depths of the dungeon. But nobody ever bothered to ask how it felt.

The Hex and the Oxen

IN THE DAYS GONE BY, when hex women and witch doctors had things their way in Pennsylvania — particularly around the Blue Mountains — there lived in those parts a farmer and his wife who loved gold more than they loved God. Sure, that farmer woman was a witch! There was no question about it, and there wasn't a thing she wouldn't do to add to her pile of gold. She'd shortweigh butter and cheese, and she would lie about the age of her chickens; she'd fill the bottom of her apple bushels with straw and lie about the hay — she wouldn't stop at anything to feel the clinking of money in her hands. She and her husband.

Folks soon found out which way the wind blew, and none would buy or barter with them. None would even speak to them. So they lived by themselves, and no gold was coming in.

One early morning they sat outside on the porch talking. Said Katie, the woman, "I miss the clinking of money in my hands."

"I miss it too," said her husband Ludwig. "But no one will buy anything from us or even speak to us."

"But we fooled them for a long time, didn't we?" said she, and both had a good laugh.

"And I'll fool them more," she added. "I have studied the hexing books I found in the old barn, and I have the devil's power. Soon the yellow gold and white silver will roll again into our hands."

"You always had a smart head on you, Katie."

"Well, good husband, I'll show you the kind of head I really have. Before night we'll have plenty of money again."

She mumbled magic words and made circles. . . . A wind blew up — and Ludwig, the farmer with the red beard, was a fine, fat, sleek brown ox! Sleek as if he had been fed the finest grain and hay.

Katie ran to neighbors and told everybody she

had a fine, strong ox for sale. Before the sun stood
in the middle of the sky, farmers and butchers
came to look at the beast.

"That ox has lived on the fat of the land," the
butcher man said.

"So he has," Katie replied.

"Where is Ludwig?" another one asked.

"Gone to Lebanon to look for more good cattle."

A man bought the animal and started home,
feeling he had struck a good bargain.

Ox and man walked on the sunny-spotted road
high up in the Blue Mountains. They reached the
top, and there was a sight fit for paradise. The man
stopped to see the broad valleys and the tidy farms,
when a wind blew up. He turned around . . . the
ox was gone!

He ran up and he ran down and he ran all
around, but all his running did him little good —
that ox was gone. And a man was walking down
the road.

He got others to help him search, but no ox
could be found. In the end he went home cursing
the hour he had bought the beast.

In the evening Katie and Ludwig were sitting
by the candlelight, counting the good money paid
for the ox.

"It was so easy to fool that fellow," Katie said.

"You are a very smart woman, and I don't mind being an ox for a little while," Ludwig said.

Time went by, and then these two thought they'd like to feel some nice hard money in their horny hands again.

"Ludwig, my pet, we'll play the same little trick. I'll use my hex and fool the fools again."

She mumbled magic words and made circles. . . . A wind blew up — and there was the sleekest, fattest white ox you ever did see. As fine an ox as ever there was in all the Blue Mountains of Pennsylvania.

Katie ran around, far and wide, and soon all knew she had a fine white ox for sale.

Men came and looked, and they said they'd never seen a finer animal. Katie asked little, and a sale was quickly made, and the man went off with his ox.

He went up the mountain. . . . A wind blew up . . . and the ox was gone!

He searched high, he searched low, and he searched all around, but it did him little good. There was no ox to be seen. But a man was walking down the road.

He told his friends the tale, and folks shook their heads and said it was ill luck to buy anything from the hex woman on the mountain.

Weeks went by, sun and moon rolled around, and one morning Katie and Ludwig missed again the clinking of money in their horny hands.

"We'll make more soon," she cried. She made a circle, mumbled words . . . a wind blew up, and there stood a fine, fat, black ox. Then she ran everywhere and told folks she had the finest black ox for sale that was ever seen. Butchers and farmers came to see, but with wary eyes.

It truly was the finest, fattest, black ox ever seen, and a butcher man from Lebanon bought it. He tied a rope around the animal's head and started homeward. But this butcher was smart! He'd brought a friend with him to keep watch.

The two had gone a ways when the Lebanon butcher man said to his friend:

"I'll drive the ox ahead. You follow a little ways behind. Don't take your eyes off that animal whatever happens. That ox'll not disappear this time."

When they got to the hill, a wild wind blew up and the ox ran off — and the butcher's friend saw, coming from the thicket, red-bearded Ludwig. . . .

"Where did you come from?" the butcher man asked.

Ludwig hemmed and hawed and mumbled and didn't know what to say.

Then the Lebanon man knew the truth.

"Your wife is a hex!" he cried. "She hexed you to become an ox and then changed you back, to cheat me! I'll have her before the judge and see her burn as a witch."

Ludwig ran off, and the butcher man went to court. He accused Katie of hexing her husband into an ox just long enough to sell him, and then changing him back, to cheat folks out of their hard-earned money.

Well, the judge made Katie and Ludwig pay back all the money they had taken. But no one could prove that Katie was a witch, so he had to let her go free. But he warned her against ever hexing in the Blue Mountains again.

Very soon after that, Katie and Ludwig moved away. And for all we know, Katie may still be hexing people somewhere in the mountains today.